HALF-MINUTE HORRORS

"Only have a minute to be scared? This is your book. Writing just a paragraph or a page, some of the best-loved kids' book authors each contributed a compact creepy tale to this collection. A definite spook-fest." —*Washington Post*

"This one's a creepy keeper." —ALA *Booklist*

"Featuring a who's who of authors and artists, this collection of more than seventy chilling snippets is ideal for campfires and car trips. The stories range from darkly humorous to outright creepy. These are inherently quick reads, but with enough plot and detail to encourage further imagining." —*Publishers Weekly*

"*Half-Minute Horrors* is the perfect choice for that smirking child who disdains fiction starring happy puppies or home-run heroes." —*School Library Journal*

"In a hurry for your horror? *Half-Minute Horrors* offers drive-thru drama. Readers will relish flipping through to find favorites and savoring tasty plotlines for later retelling." —*The Bulletin of the Center for Children's Books*

HALF-MINUTE HORRORS

HALF-MINUTE

HOR

RORS

EDITED BY
SUSAN RICH

HARPER

An *Imprint of* HarperCollins*Publishers*

"A Thousand Faces" by Brian Selznick first appeared in *The Boy of a Thousand Faces*, published by HarperCollins Children's Books in 2000. Printed here by permission of the author.

"The Shadow" by Neil Gaiman was previously broadcast on Weekend America's Halloween Radio program in 2007. Printed here by permission of the author.

Half-Minute Horrors
Copyright © 2009 by HarperCollins Publishers, Inc.
All rights reserved. Printed in the United States of America.
No part of this book may be used or reproduced in any manner
whatsoever without written permission except in the case of brief
quotations embodied in critical articles and reviews. For information
address HarperCollins Children's Books, a division of HarperCollins
Publishers, 10 East 53rd Street, New York, NY 10022.
www.harpercollinschildrens.com

Library of Congress Cataloging-in-Publication Data
Half-minute horrors / edited by Susan Rich. — 1st ed.
          p.   cm.
Summary: An anthology of very short, scary stories by an assortment of
authors and illustrators including Chris Raschka, Joyce Carol Oates, Neil Gaiman,
Jack Gantos, and Lane Smith.
      ISBN 978-0-06-183381-6
      1. Children's stories.   2. Horror tales.   [1. Horror stories.   2. Short stories.]
I. Rich, Susan, date
PZ5.H147   2009   2009018293
[Fic]—dc22   CIP
                                                                      AC
Typography by Torborg Davern
11   12   13   14   15   CG/CW   10 9 8 7 6 5 4 3 2 1
❖
First paperback edition, 2011

Table of
Contents

HALF-MINUTE
HORRORS

LEMONY SNICKET

Something You Ought to Know

"The right hand doesn't know what the left is doing" is a phrase that refers to times when people ought to know, but don't know, about something that is happening very close to them. For instance, you ought to know about the man who watches you when you sleep.

He is a quiet man, which is why you don't know about him.

You don't know how he gets into your home, or how he finds his way to the room in which you sleep. You don't know how he can stare at you so long without blinking, and you don't know how he manages to be gone by morning, without a trace, and you don't know where he purchased the long, sharp knife, curved like a crescent moon, that he holds in his left hand, sometimes just millimeters from your eyes, which are closed and flickering in dreams.

There are, of course, things he does not know about you, either. He does not know what you are dreaming about, but then it may be that he does not care. His clothes are rumpled and have odd rips in them here and there. One of his coat sleeves is longer than the other, and this may be to cover his right hand. The sleeve is long enough that if you were to wake up and see him, which you never do, you might not see that his right hand is strange and crooked. It would take a while, in the darkness of the room, to notice that it is missing three fingers.

He comes every night. His right hand does not know what the left is doing.

JERRY SPINELLI

The Chicken or the Egg

"I was first," said Egg.

"I was first," said Chicken.

"I was," said Egg.

"I was," said Chicken.

"I was!"

"I was!"

"I was!"

"I was!"

"Okay," said Chicken. "You win." And pecked Egg. Seven times. From seven holes Egg bled yellow into the barnyard dust. Until all of Egg was out instead of in.

Chicken grinned. "But guess who's last."

KENNETH OPPEL

In Hiding

My father and I lay tensely side by side in total darkness, not daring to breathe. The space was small and smelled bad. We were flat on our backs, scarcely able to lift our heads. Above us, the thing shifted restlessly on its bed, grunting. I hoped it would settle itself soon.

Finally the thing stopped moving. I counted seconds. Was it asleep? Or just lying there awake, waiting?

"Now," my father whispered in my ear.

And very slowly we reached out and up to grasp the child's ankles with our cold, dead hands.

THE OLD MAN IN THE PICTURE

by R. SALA

Jake's mother promised him that if he sat quietly in the waiting room while she saw her new doctor, he could have three bowls of ice cream afterward.

Despite the promise, Jake was not happy. He didn't like waiting, and he didn't like the room.

He especially didn't like that ugly portrait of an old man hanging on the wall across from where he sat.

Jake didn't like that the old man seemed to be staring right at him with a strange and awful look.

Jake tried moving, but the eyes of the old man seemed to follow him around the room.

It was a creepy picture, all right, but Jake wasn't scared. No, not in the least. He marched right up to that picture and...

That's when he suddenly noticed the old man's hands.

They were bony and scaly and had long, pointed nails.

When his mother finally came out of the doctor's office, there was no sign of Jake.

Although she did glimpse an old man slipping out the door.

He looked oddly familiar....

Then she turned around and looked at the portrait.

And her screams could be heard all the way down the street.

~END

ERIN HUNTER

The Babysitter

The phone rang, echoing around the white-and-silver kitchen that was as glossy as a hall of mirrors. Jess was surrounded by a dozen reflections of herself as she went to pick up the handset.

"Hello?"

For a moment there was no answer, just the faint sound of someone breathing. Jess thought of her friends laughing as they told her not to accept the babysitting job from someone she'd never met. "They probably live in a creepy old house in the middle of the woods!"

They didn't. They lived in a top-floor loft with a view of the city that made Jess feel like a bird. The white leather sofas smelled of plastic wrapping.

Then a little voice said, "I'm coming home," before the line clicked off.

Was there another child Jess didn't know about?

The phone rang again. "I'm coming home!" Now the voice sounded old, tired, and fretful. There was a tap of footsteps. Climbing marble stairs. Like the ones that led up to the loft.

Jess looked down. Something was brushing her leg. It was the phone cord. It had fallen out of the wall.

The sound of scratching at the door. Like a dog. In her hand, the phone rang. "I'm home!" rasped the voice, older than sand. "Did you wait up?"

JAMES PATTERSON

Grand Entrance

Here's what I remember about that night, and though I've been told it's not possible, I remember everything clearly, like a dream come to life. . . .

I felt trapped. There was terrible screaming.

Where am I? I wondered. Some kind of tightly enclosed space.

My fear was extreme. I tried to stay calm, but I couldn't.

There was water everywhere around me.

The screaming kept getting louder. And closer.

Then a voice broke through.

"It's a girl," said the voice.

Suddenly, it was quiet. Another voice filled the room. I realized it was mine.

And I was screaming like a baby.

SONYA SONES

Halloween Mask

I am me,
but I am not.

I can't be sure
whose face feels hot.

Is it mine?
Or is it its?

So strange how snug
this new mask fits. . . .

Gazing in the mirror
over my sink,

staring into eyes
that refuse to blink,

holding my ground,
I stare right back

at eyes the deadest
shade of black. . . .

I swallow hard.
This can't be true—

when last I looked,
my eyes

were blue!

TOM GENRICH & MICHÈLE PERRY

Tenton

Father said stuffed toys were childish. But at nine Ava still adored hers, most of all Tenton, the white rat. Tenton had velvety fur worn thin and long tickly whiskers, and traveled with her between Mom's place and here. No matter what Ava's fear, Tenton always knew how to comfort her.

One evening Father, as usual, nodded good night to Ava and closed the bedroom door. She heard his chair whine as he sat down to work again.

Shadows slowly lengthened into night. Under the covers Ava whispered, "I don't ever want to go back to school. I hate it!" Something drove her to add, "*You* go, Tenton. You take my place." Tenton's red eyes glittered.

The next thing Ava knew, she was being tossed into the air like a rag doll. She hit the carpet yet felt nothing.

In the half-light she saw a creature leap out of bed, a girl of sorts with shiny pale hair, *her* hair, wearing a pendant necklace, *her* necklace—but a girl who moved like a rat, scurrying stealthily on all fours. Ava screamed: no sound. She scrambled: no movement.

The girl-size rat crept over, red eyes deep with malice. Reflected in them Ava saw a little stuffed toy flung aside on the carpet, white limbs a-tangle, blue eyes wide with panic. *Ava's* blue eyes.

The rat hissed and raced to the open window. A long naked tail snaked over the sill; claws clicked down the trellis. Then the sounds of movement faded.

In the morning Ava heard Father's alarm, his shuffling footsteps. "Ava!" he grunted. "Get up, or you'll be late! *Ava!*"

Ava did what she could. Which was nothing.

ANGELA JOHNSON

Nanny

My nanny, Sara, tucks me in as the shadows wait for her to leave so they can creep out of the closet toward me. She smiles as she steps over the books and puzzle pieces I've left on the floor, then closes my door.

But tonight I decide to escape the shadows. I open the door and dash toward Sara's room, only to find her at the end of the hall, whispering to them—the shadows—and telling them with a smile that I was waiting for their nightly visit to my room.

THE LEGEND OF ALEXANDRA & ROSE

BY JON KLASSEN

LEGEND:

1. ALEXANDRA'S ROOM WITH THE SMALL WINDOW
2. ROSE'S ROOM WITH THE BIGGER WINDOW
3. TOOLSHED
4. 5. 6. 7. ROSE
2. ALEXANDRA'S ROOM WITH THE BIGGER WINDOW

ARTHUR SLADE

What's Coming

My father always used to say you'll get what's coming to you and I really didn't like know what he meant until like this moment right now 'cause I can't even move my arms and my chest it's the pressure you see I'd decided to slip into old Widow Sturm's house and I stole the heavy silver candlesticks and quiet as a rat I snuck back out the basement climbing over this container with old wood on top it's for catching rain oh yeah it's a cistern and the wood broke and I fell into this pit that just has thick slimy mud inside and I keep sinking and as it reaches my nostrils I start to bubble and I can't help but wonder is it the candlesticks that keep pulling me down

M. T. ANDERSON

An Easy Gig

Galv thought the Kennedys' baby was being very good. He didn't hear a peep from the kid all night. As baby-sitting gigs go, it was incredibly easy. The baby was already down for the night when he arrived. So Galv watched TV and talked to Raoul on the phone and ate the lasagna the Kennedy parents had left in the oven for him.

He did not check the baby's room to make sure the baby was still sleeping. He didn't check the crib to make sure the baby was even still there.

He lay on the sofa with his head hanging off the armrest and his lasagna plate on his stomach, making up song lyrics with Raoul. They laughed hard.

And when the parents came home and said, "How was the baby?" Galv said, "Oh, he was good. Really good. I didn't even hear a peep from him."

But Galv didn't know how the baby was. He hadn't checked.

"No," said Mr. Kennedy. "The baby was bad."

"Very bad," said Mrs. Kennedy. "The baby cried and cried."

"No he didn't," said Galv, confused.

"Before you got here," Mr. Kennedy explained. "The baby was so bad he had to be punished."

"And when we punished him," said Mrs. Kennedy, "we made a mistake."

"And then," said Mr. Kennedy, "we needed somewhere to hide the body. And someone to blame."

Galv backed toward the door, terrified. He couldn't speak.

"You can't run from it," said Mrs. Kennedy. "The police will never believe you. The crime is already yours."

Mr. Kennedy smiled. "How did you like the lasagna?" he said.

YVONNE PRINZ

Mr. Black

Every morning at seven sharp, my next-door neighbor emerges from the front door of his house. He has no wife, no kids, and no dog. He disappears up the street on foot wearing a black suit, black shoes, and a black hat, and carrying a black briefcase. We call him Mr. Black. One day my curiosity gets the better of me and I peek into his living room window. Through a crack in the blinds I see that it is not a living room at all. It's a waiting room. Five more Mr. Blacks sit in a row of plastic chairs, not moving, not blinking, not breathing. I hear a whirr, and a small camera mounted up in the far corner of the room swivels and focuses in on me. A red light blinks. I run.

M. E. KERR

The Foot Dragger

My father thought the reason my older brother was mean was that he was short. He'd grow out of it.

When he came in late at night, while my parents were asleep, I would hear him heading toward our bedrooms. He would drag one foot and take his time climbing the stairs.

Step . . . drag . . . step . . . drag. Heavy breathing. The door handle turned.

I decided two could play this game. As the handle turned, I'd jump out at him. I was ready for him. *Step . . . drag.* The heavy breathing. He was there.

"Gotcha, Paul!" I threw open the door and saw him.

This very tall man.

TRICK

WE'RE NOT SUPPOSED TO TRICK or TREAT THE HOUSES WITH NO LIGHTS ON.

CAN'T HURT TO CHECK.

CREEEEEE

The door was answered by a man dressed all in black. Like a ninja. He had a sack, too.

TRICK or TREAT!

OH, RIGHT.

I FORGOT. LET ME SEE.

HERE. A PRETTY BROOCH FOR THE LITTLE MERMAID, AND A GOLDEN CANDLESTICK FOR THE VAMPIRE.

WOW. THANKS.

WE THOUGHT MAYBE NOBODY WAS HOME.

NOBODY IS,

the man replied...

...and he ran off down the street with his sack full of treats.

aDam rEX 2009

DEAN LOREY

Hank

Hank was one of the most adorable puppies you've ever seen, which is why it was such a shock when, seven years after the day we brought him home from the pet store, he looked up at me with his big, beautiful Labrador eyes and said, "I'm going to kill you."

"You . . . you can talk?" I whispered.

"Of course, dummy. I just haven't talked to *you* until right now."

I was alone in the house with him. It was a freedom I gained on my thirteenth birthday—a freedom I suddenly regretted.

"I haven't decided exactly *how* I'm going to do it yet," Hank continued, stepping closer on his padded feet. Drool dripped from his long front teeth. "I was going to tear into your throat while you were sleeping, but I think I may just go ahead and do it right now."

"But . . . but I thought you loved me," I replied, stumbling backward. "I thought we were best friends!"

"I know. What a dummy you are." He laughed cheerlessly. "Yeah, every time I licked you, you know what I was thinking? I was thinking, *I'm gonna kill him.* Lick. *Make him suffer.* Lick, lick. *Watch him die in front of me with that scared, confused look in his eyes.*

"You thought that when we were snuggling?" I reached behind me. My hands closed around a lamp—a weapon, maybe? "I had no idea . . ."

"I know," Hank said before attacking.

SARAH WEEKS

One of a Kind

When I felt the first tug, I knew I had something big on the line.

"Ka-ching!" I thought.

People pay big bucks for fresh tuna, and big bucks was exactly what I needed. I'd spent a wad on Gloria's engagement ring—way more than I could afford—but love makes a man do crazy things sometimes.

"One of a kind," the guy at the jewelry store had told me when he showed me the diamond ring.

"Perfect," I said, "'cause that's what my Gloria is. One of a kind."

It took me a good half hour to reel in the fish. It put up quite a fight. But when it finally broke the surface of the water, my heart sank.

"Mako," I said when I saw the gray fin.

Shark meat wouldn't bring in nearly as much as tuna, but I pulled the fish into the boat anyway. After stomping on the head a couple of times with my boot heel to stun it, I took a knife and starting at the throat, sliced downward, opening up the gut. The usual fish heads and stomach juice spilled out onto the deck, but then something sparkled and caught my eye. There amid the slimy stomach contents lay a hand, a woman's left hand, and on the second finger was a ring. It was one of a kind.

GLORIA WHELAN

A Walk Too Far

I had walked too far, ending up in a neighborhood of homes with a deserted look. The streetlights came on, and I hurried from one pale pool of light to the next, searching for something familiar.

At last, admitting I was lost, I approached a house where the flick of a curtain suggested it was occupied. Hoping for directions, I knocked at the door.

The man who answered my knock appeared strangely pleased to see me, as though he had been waiting for me, or someone like me, to appear. He ushered me into a darkened room.

"So then no one knows you are here," the man said.

I heard a key turn in a lock.

HOLLY BLACK

A Very Short Story

Zoe sits on the bed, with her mother at the foot. The overhead light is on, flooding most of the room, although shadows still creep up the walls at the edges.

"Sit with me until I fall asleep," Zoe says.

There is a party going on downstairs. Zoe's mother hesitates. She can hear the clink of glasses, the bursts of low laughter. She's restless, longing to be down there, but Zoe will just sit alone in her brightly lit bed and wait for her mother to come back and finish the ritual. Zoe won't sleep otherwise.

"Okay," Zoe's mother says. "Get under the covers."

Zoe snuggles down under them. "Tell me why vampires can't get me."

"Vampires can't come in unless they're invited," Zoe's mother says, as she always does.

"What about werewolves?"

Zoe's mother makes a show of looking through the curtains. "No full moon tonight."

Zoe's eyes drift closed, but she's far from sleeping. She has a new question, one she's just thought up. "What about ghosts?"

Her mother pauses, looking down at her hands. Finally she answers. "Ghosts don't want to hurt anyone. If they hurt you, they do it by accident."

"What if they hurt me by accident then?" Zoe says, looking up at her mother.

"They can only hurt the living," says Zoe's mother, her voice soft.

"Oh," says Zoe.

After a few moments, Zoe is asleep. Zoe's mother leans down to kiss her good night, but it's like kissing smoke.

FAYE KELLERMAN

Deep Six

When I started to say something witty, Babe interrupted. "We're not interested, Tubby. The only reason we're here is because you have the pool."

She swung her magnificent waist-length blond hair in my face.

"You should wear a bathing cap, you know."

She laughed. "Yeah, I could also be a dork like you, Tubbs."

"My name is Tabitha," I said under my breath. I ran my hand through the warm eddies of the Jacuzzi. I wasn't fat. I was Rubenesque. It's just that morons like Babe were anorexic.

I hated her. She tortured me whenever she had an audience—which was all the time. The only reason I put up with her was because everywhere she went, she brought all the good-looking boys.

"Jacuzzi, anyone?" Babe asked as she stepped into the whirling water. "Get out of the way, Tubbs. We need the space."

"No problem."

My hand went to the safety cap of the intake valve, and I slowly loosened it until it dropped to the floor. It took only a few seconds for Babe's hair to catch, her pouty lips forming an "O," her eyes wide-open as she was sucked underwater. Everyone started to scream, but I was somewhere else.

Serves her right. She should have worn a bathing cap.

the TURN of the SCREW

BY HENRY JAMES,
A NOVEL
AS TOLD by
LISA BROWN
in FEWER THAN
30 SECONDS.

the GOVERNESS SEES GHOSTS...

OR PERHAPS SHE IS *Insane.*

EITHER WAY,
IT'S QUITE SCARY.

PSEUDONYMOUS BOSCH

The Attack of the
Flying Mustaches

They descended on the boys of St. S——'s in a dark cloud, swarming like locusts. Up close, they were terrifying. Quivering, bristling animals without eyes or ears. Each mustache hair seemed to move by itself, a teeny tiny tentacle with a mind of its own. Some landed on the boys' backs or chests. Some between the boys' eyebrows. But most found their targets under the boys' noses. There they dug in like so many flying leeches, irritating the boys' nostrils and feeding off the boys' blood and snot. They did not leave until years later, when they were gray and crusty and the boys were dead.

NADIA AGUIAR

Takowanda

When Sam and his father moved alone to remote Takowanda Island, hundreds of miles from anywhere, Sam found that there were hardly any children there. Left to amuse himself, he wandered the empty beach and the garden, at the end of which was the biggest tree he had ever seen. Its branches were too deep and too thick with leaves to see very far inside it, and its top was often lost in the clouds. The great, noisy, oil-colored Takowanda birds with their watchful eyes and razor-sharp half-moon beaks lived in it.

"Don't go near that tree," the fat-armed lady with the wide-set eyes who came to cook for them told Sam. "You know what Takowanda means? It means devil. D-E-V-I-L. Those is the devil's birds."

"Silly local superstition. Pay it no mind," said Sam's

father later. The birds watched them. *Takowanda, Takowanda, Takowanda,* they sang.

On a sweltering, airless summer afternoon Sam was alone in the backyard when he heard children's laughter. He ran to the end of the garden, but the dirt track that ran past the house was empty. He heard the laughter again, and he peered into the thick green tree, but there was no one.

"Hello!" he called. Nothing. "Hello!"

His heart sank—he had been so happy at the thought of finding someone his own age. But there it was again—someone *was* laughing! Sam realized the sound was coming from above him, high in the branches of the great tree. He looked up, but the leaves were too thick to see through. What he did see, though, were almost perfect hand- and footholds carved into the trunk. Sam began to climb. He went higher and higher, following the laughter. He looked down once, and the earth was far below. But he kept going, up, up, up through the lofty green heights, into the moss and shadow of the dark world inside the tree. He was deep within it when he caught sight of something that made him freeze—a single child's shoe, dangling from a branch just above him, its laces tangled, its leather old and cracked. In a sudden cold rush, Sam saw what had been around him all along: small children's skeletons, hanging from the crooks of branches, bones picked clean, held together only with scraps of faded clothes—and all around them the heavy black bodies of hundreds of roosting Takowanda birds, motionless and silent.

One of the birds opened its razor-sharp beak, and once again Sam heard the child's laugh. Then the whole flock opened their beaks to chant. *Takowanda, Takowanda, Takowanda*, they began softly, their voices rising as they crept down the branches toward him.

All around the island and out across the ocean echoed the strident, victorious cry:

Takowanda, Takowanda, Takowanda!

SIENNA MERCER

Heart Stopper

My camp counselor sniffled. "My grams always said that if you fall into freezing cold water, your heart will stop." She peered down at the dark water.

"It was so terrible," her voice whispered.

The two of us stood on the dock, huddled together for warmth in our doubled-up socks. It was the first time I'd been this close to the water since Sherri died. It had been two days, and the same odd, wintry chill still hadn't lifted from the lake.

I put my head on my counselor's shoulder. She'd been the person closest to the accident when it happened.

"You should have heard her scream," my counselor said, her chest heaving. I shivered. We'd all heard it up on Girls' Camp, but I didn't want to correct her. I'd thought it was the strangled howl of an animal being attacked.

"It wasn't your fault," I said, trying to comfort her.

My counselor didn't say anything. Finally I lifted my head, and I saw that she was grinning.

My mouth flew open, and she shoved me off the dock with her palms wide-open.

JACK GANTOS

Up to My Elbow

I had done some bad things but went to bed without regrets, and that night I thought the welt on the palm of my hand was a bug bite and so I scratched it, but the next morning it had grown red and puffy and cracked open like tiny lips, and when I grabbed my school backpack it hurt, but it was a hurt that was like wanting to cry when someone is cruel to you. I pulled a glove down over my hand and suddenly shuddered from the panicked feeling in my chest as if being locked in a closet. I yanked the glove off and took a deep breath. What is going on? I asked myself. I twisted the doorknob to leave the house but instead dropped to my knees with overwhelming shame. "Oh my God," I wailed, "what have I done?" I looked into my stinging hand, and the little lips were whispering, "What you feel is now who you are. Get used to it." What else could I do? The choice was clear. I ran up to the kitchen for a knife.

STEPHEN MARCHE

Four Gleams in the Moonlight

The first gleam was the deer's eye as I swerved to avoid it, crashing my car into the ditch. The deer fled like a shadow.

The second gleam was the light from the house across the field, in the first thick part of the woods, which I headed for, in search of a telephone.

I knocked. I could see a lovely table set for two in the kitchen through the window. A man with a crooked smile opened the door (his bright, crooked teeth were the third gleam). He ushered me in with a sweep of his hand.

Then everything went black.

When I awoke, I was lying on the kitchen table set for two. The moonlight streamed through the window like a scarf, but I couldn't see a thing. I couldn't move my hands or feet.

A blade flashed: the fourth gleam in the moonlight.

BRAD MELTZER

The Goblin Book

On his deathbed, my grandfather gave me *The Goblin Book*.

"It'll work for you," he whispered. "It will."

Don't worry. I was confused too. I didn't like creepy old grandfathers who talked in riddles. It was annoying.

But he explained how it worked. How a reader—usually a smart one—would be holding a book, lost in a story. And then the book would feel odd in the reader's hands.

The book would feel heavy, then lighter, then heavy again.

And then the reader would have the oddest feeling of all: that inescapable feeling that someone was watching them.

It was true, of course. That was the gift of *The Goblin Book*. With it, I could find any reader . . . and watch

them through their book.
    The best part?
    I can see you right now.
    I can.
    No, you think to yourself.
    But I can. And I'll see you again tonight.

WORMS

Do you ever think when the hearse goes by, that you might be the next to die?

**AND ALL GOES WELL,
FOR ABOUT A WEEK,
AND THEN YOUR COFFIN,
BEGINS TO LEAK.**

They put you in a black pine box,
Then cover you up with dirt and rocks.

The worms crawl in, the worms crawl out,
The worms play pinochle on your snout.

They eat your eyes, they eat your nose,
They eat the jam between your toes.

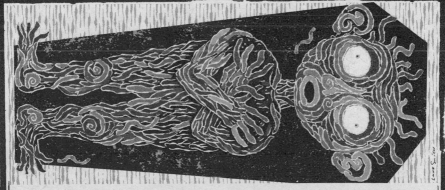

And when your bones decay and rot, the worms are left but you are not.

CAROL GORMAN

The Dare

"I dare you," Jack said. "Knock on the door and ask for a drink."

Tommy touched his red cap with a shaky hand, climbed the rotted porch steps, and knocked.

The door creaked open and Tommy stepped inside. Through the lighted window, Jack saw him sit on the couch.

"He never came out," Jack told his dad later as they approached the dark house.

"The place has been abandoned for years," his dad said. "See?"

They climbed the steps and pushed open the front door. Their flashlight lit only cobwebs in the empty room.

"Must've been some other house," his dad said. "He'll be home soon." They closed the door behind them.

Neither saw the red cap lying in the dusty corner.

DAVID RICH

The Ballad of John Grepsy

Oh campers, young and tender,
In tents and cabins sleeping,
While you sleep out in the deep woods,
Something's out there creeping.

You hear the wind a-howling
Like spirits lost and lonely
And angry ghosts, whose whispers boast,
"I'm coming for you only."

You're on the land
That once was mine.
There's only you to blame.
My blade is keen, my spirits mean—
John Grepsy is my name.

My name is John Grepsy, John Grepsy, John Grepsy.
Remember this name all your life.
Remember with fright that on some overnight
I'll be there with my sharp hunting knife.

So when the moon's in shadows
Long after night descends,
My curse comes quick when fog is thick,
When dark with darkness blends.

Remember me, John Grepsy,
As you're lying in your bed.
While you sleep, that's when I'll creep,
And then you'll all be dead.

JENNY NIMMO

Soup

I wish someone had warned me about Alice's soup.
  I'll never get rid of these horns now.
  Baaa!

MARGARET ATWOOD

The Creeping Hand

The hand crept up the cellar stairs. It was shriveled and dirty, and its fingernails were long.

It scuttled along the dark hallway. At the closed door it sniffed with its fingertips, then jumped up like a giant spider, grabbed the doorknob, and turned.

Inside the room it found a sock. Then a shoe. And then—another hand, hanging down from the bed. A young hand, a hand that it could kidnap and take away down to the cellar.

But this hand was attached to an arm.

Something could be done about that.

MARIKO TAMAKI

Wet Sand, Little Teeth

The hole was about four feet deep and three feet wide. And mostly, you know, it was just a hole this girl Jenny from three cottages over found.

Jenny said she saw someone digging the hole, although she didn't know why someone would, like, create this big hole, then just leave it there. I'd never seen anyone walking around with a shovel, but Jenny said she saw a guy. In some ways, the hole appeared almost as mysteriously as Jenny, who just sort of showed up on our porch one day, looking for snacks and someone to play with.

"Wow, that kid sure is little for someone who eats so much," my dad used to say. "She looks like a lemur."

Mom said to ignore Dad. "It's good she finally gets someone her age up here after all her wishing."

It may seem strange, but playing in the hole with Jenny

was really fun. Jenny had a million games that involved a hole in the sand.

The hole itself was kind of cool. Every day, Jenny and I found some new weird thing pushed into the sand in the bottom. One time it was this pile of teeth Jenny said were "small white stones" (but they were pointy). Once it was a chewed-up flip-flop.

We would play there, together, all day, until about the time when it started getting dark. As soon as there was a hint of not sunshine anymore, Jenny would always find some reason to get out of the hole, typically by demanding that it was time to go get a Popsicle at my place.

"You can't stay here. . . . I mean, we can't stay in here," she'd always insist. "Get out of the hole."

Jenny was a bit bossy.

I don't exactly remember all the things that happened on that day in August. At some point, Jenny and I were fighting about something, by which I mean that Jenny probably wanted something and I wouldn't give it to her.

That evening, when the sun started to set, Jenny jumped out of the hole and said I should stay.

"Stay," she whispered as she crawled out. "Go ahead."

At first, nothing happened. Then the dark started spreading over the sand and sank into the hole.

That's when I felt it. Something touching me. Like a

finger. At first I thought it was a sand toad.

"Uh, Jenny?"

Then there was a sound, like a swallow in reverse. Gravelly. Then it grabbed me, grabbed my feet, something with strong scratchy hands.

I kicked one foot free. Tried to reach out to Jenny, but she was walking away.

I watched her disappear, watched her feet as I grabbed for the edge of the hole, which I couldn't really grab because it was sand.

Then the something grabbed my shoulder.

And I took a breath and it felt like a hammer in my throat. And I blacked out.

When I woke up, my mom was wrapping me in a beach towel. My dad was holding a flashlight, looking at me.

"What's that on her shoulder?" Mom screamed.

A mark. Like little teeth.

We still don't know what it is.

Now I'm not allowed to play with Jenny or the hole. Dad filled it up. Just as well I guess. Jenny's a jerk.

BRIAN SELZNICK

A Thousand Faces

FRANCINE PROSE

Chocolate Cake

Lately, I've had the definite feeling that my parents aren't my parents. I can't exactly explain it. But I'm convinced that they're space aliens who look and act like my parents and have taken their places.

I've been asking them trick questions to trip them up. "Dad, what was the name of my first puppy?"

"Uh . . . Fluffy?"

"His name was Earnest," I say.

"I've got a lot on my mind," says "Dad."

Tonight I'm trying something new. My real mom is horribly allergic to chocolate. She breaks out in a skin rash if she even looks at chocolate.

I bake my fake mom a chocolate birthday cake. I watch her eat it. No rash. She smiles.

"Delicious," she says. "Thank you, Timmy."

"My name is Jimmy," I say.

AYELET WALDMAN

At the Water's Edge

The water is still, and so clear I can see the tangled stems of the lily pads leading down to the muddy bottom. I have made a careful study of the lilies, their white outer leaves that shade to pale pink and finally to magenta. The pistils are bright orange, the color of the dress my mother was wearing when she left for work this morning, only a few minutes before the children came. I am paying such close attention to the blossoms floating in the pond because I don't want to look at the children. The pond is small, and they have surrounded it entirely. They stand very still, staring at me. I think they don't even blink, but since I try to avoid their eyes, I cannot really tell. They don't say a word.

It has been hours since they first burst through the doors and crawled through the windows, silent all the while, even when they snatched my little sister from her crib and bundled her away. My mother should be home by now.

They have never once spoken, or shouted, even when I managed to tear loose from their filthy hands and race out to the pond. They chased me, their fingers brushing the edges of my clothes. I leaped into the canoe and paddled out to the middle of the pond, a smart thing to do, it turned out, since it seems they cannot swim. But the pond is shallow, and soon enough they'll figure out that they can wade. Already I see one or two of them testing the water with their dirt-encrusted toes.

I hear the noise of an engine, and only now do I allow myself to burst into tears. My mother is home—her car is coming up the driveway. She will chase them away. Except the car door is opening and it is not my mother who is stepping out. It is one of the children, dirty and disheveled, with torn clothes and bare feet. I am staring at the child who has replaced my mother, and there is no air left in my lungs. The child lifts her hand and waves.

It will be dark soon.

R.L. STINE

My Worst Nightmare

For a long time, I had the terrifying idea that an evil stranger lived in my bedroom closet. It was my worst nightmare.

My room was up in the attic. It was a long, narrow room. My bed was against one wall. My closet stood at the far wall. It was as big as a room. The kind of closet you can walk in. I kept the white wooden door shut tight.

Late at night, I'd hear noises in the closet. Bumps and soft thumps.

I knew a stranger was hiding in there. Living secretly in our house. When I told my parents, they laughed at me and told me to grow up.

One night, the noises in the closet were loud and frightening. *Thump thump bump.* Was someone moving around in there?

No *way* I could get to sleep. I knew I had to look.

My legs trembled as I stepped up to the closet door. My hand shook as I reached for the knob.

Thump bump thump.

I took a deep breath—and pulled open the door. And let out a moan of horror.

Deep in the closet, a red-haired boy stared back at me. "NO! OH, NO!" he screamed. "I *knew* someone was hiding in my closet . . . living in my house! It's my *worst nightmare!*"

ADELE GRIFFIN

The Beast Outside

Jane didn't say thank you for the dollhouse. She just began to destroy it.

"Twister!" She smashed the furniture. The dolls hid in the attic. They were used to children who loved them.

Did Mama cry out when Jane tore her dress? Did the Boy bruise when she hurled him down the stairs? Jane grinned, locked Granny and her Scottie in the trunk, and shoved Papa up the chimney.

After Twister, Jane played Flood. Typhoon. Famine. She ripped off Mama's leg and set it on a plate. "Eat that!"

The next morning, Jane saw what the dolls had done. The Boy lay in a heap as if thrown from the roof. Inside, Papa hung from a noose, his neck snapped. Granny'd stuck her head in the oven. Mama was drowned in the tub.

A growl made Jane jump. The Scottie's eyeball filled her window.

Time to play Revenge.

Unannounced

"Hi," Allan said, his eyes huge and pleading. He was rain drenched, slicked wet in a T-shirt and cargo pants.

"Eight weeks after dumping me. Now you show up. Real nice."

He wiped his face. "You've been counting?"

"Leave." She wanted to close the door, slam it in his face. But he looked like he needed to say something. "What?"

He took one step inside, then back out. "I love you."

She blinked. "Great for you."

This time she had no problem shutting him out, for good.

At breakfast the next morning, her brother gently tapped her shoulder. "Emmy?"

She rubbed her eyes groggily. She had barely slept the

night before, thinking of the pleading look he'd given her, the rain coating his hair.

"Remember that kid you used to see? Allan what's-his-face?"

She opened her mouth, then closed it. "Why?"

"They found his body at the bottom of St. Peter Lake. It made the front page."

"W-what?" she stuttered. "What happened?"

He shrugged. "I don't know, Em. Paper says he'd been there for at least two months."

"But that—that's impossible."

"I'm sorry, Em. It's probably weird for you. You haven't seen him in months, and now you'll . . ."

He trailed off.

"I'll never see him again," she finished. She wondered if it was true.

The End

ALLAN STRATTON

There's Something Under the Bed

"There's something under the bed."

"Don't be silly. You're a big boy now," his father said, and turned out the light.

"But there is! Please, Daddy, look!"

So his father got down in the dark beside the bed. And disappeared.

"Daddy? . . . Where are you, Daddy?"

A gentle chuckle. "I'm under the bed."

"You sound different."

"Do I?"

"Yes. Very different. . . . Are you really Daddy?"

"Why don't you come under the bed and find out?"

SARAH L. THOMSON

Cat's Paw

The boy sat up in bed, listening.

First a feathery sound. Like a dry paintbrush whispering across paper.

Then footsteps softer than his own heartbeat.

Finally a thump more felt than heard, as something landed on the bed.

The boy groped for a lamp. He touched the switch. He looked at the cat sitting by his feet.

He sighed. "It's you. I thought it was something scary."

"Silly," said the cat. "Cats aren't scary."

"I'm dreaming," the boy whispered. "Cats can't talk!"

"I wouldn't worry about that," answered the cat. Her whiskers were wet with something sticky and dark.

"I'd worry about the rats," she added. "Now *that's* scary."

Inside the wall, the boy could hear tiny claws scrabbling at plaster.

When the claws broke through, he could swear the cat smiled.

KATHERINE APPLEGATE

Horrorku

Death's gruesome face taunts:
soulless eyes, crimson grimace.
I really hate clowns.

AVI

The Itch

It was an itch that woke me. I pulled my hand out from beneath the warm blanket and scratched my face.

I felt hair. Odd, I thought. Hadn't I shaved today?

I started to tuck my hand away when I realized it was wet. Increasingly puzzled, I turned on my bedside lamp and looked. The hand was covered with hair. And it was bloody, too. The fingernails had become yellow and long.

I leaped out of bed and ran to the bathroom. I peered into a mirror.

A wolf looked back at me. I growled, revealing my fangs.

What I felt was a great need to get outside and start hunting.

I'm not even sure I shut the door. I was that hungry.

GAIL CARSON LEVINE

The New Me: A Pantoum

This heat. I pull myself along,
blocking the narrow school stairway.
I wish for a broader chest, stronger legs.
A teacher pushes past, angry at the delay

blocking the narrow school stairway.
My skin feels tight on my bones.
A teacher pushes past, angry at the delay.
I grow heavy and as stupid as an ox.

My skin feels tight on my bones.
Jennifer says, "You okay, Sam?"
I grow heavy and as stupid as an ox,
thinking, How changed I am.

Jennifer says, "You okay, Sam?"
I shake my huge head. I'm yoked to a plow,
thinking, How changed I am.
Farmer, do not use your whip!

I shake my huge head. I'm yoked to a plow.
I wish for a broader chest, stronger legs.
Farmer, do not use your whip!
This heat. I pull myself along.

DAVID STAHLER JR.

Always Eleven

I told you last night, I won't hurt you. Not me.

Yes, the house was just as moldy and awful when we came here too. Father was dead in the war, and my little brother cried every night. But it wasn't just for missing Father. It was that man.

You know him.

He showed up not long after we got here, seemed to cast a spell over Mother. Not us. It was the way he moved. Smooth and quiet, like a slinking wolf. And he hated us. This was his house. That's what he told us.

One night, James wouldn't stop crying. The noise brought the man up to the top of the stairs, to throw open the door.

"Why are you crying?" he growled at us. "What are you afraid of?"

"Monsters," James whimpered.

"There are no monsters," I hissed. "Stop crying and go to sleep." I just wanted that man to leave, to close the door and leave us to the cold.

He didn't say anything. He just laughed. That's when I saw the eyes start their glowing, a devilish red in the darkness.

It didn't take long, what happened next.

So that's why I'm here. So many years later and I'm still here. Still eleven. Always eleven, just like you.

CARSON ELLIS

Aloft

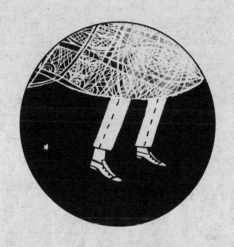

Way up in the night sky
I could swear I saw
Something moving
Above the rooftops
Weaving slowly through the trees
I thought I saw...

Someone floating

TUI T. SUTHERLAND

Skittering

I knew I never should have killed that spider.

I was making my bed when I saw something skitter away under the sheets. I threw back the blankets and slammed my book onto the mattress, banging and smashing and screaming until the big brown spider was a squashy, flat, oozing mess.

My skin was crawling. Had the spider been in the bed with me all night? I pulled all the sheets off the bed and took them to my mom, and we put them straight into the washing machine.

But even with new sheets, I couldn't sleep that night. I kept feeling tiny legs slithering over my skin. Prickly thin fingers danced across my bare feet, climbed slowly up my pajamas, brushed against my exposed neck. I thought I was imagining things. I tried to ignore it.

And then . . . I felt something as small as a pencil eraser land softly on my cheek and scuttle toward my ear.

I sat up, shrieking. I was still screaming for help when my mom came running in and turned on the light.

The ceiling was swarming with spiders. Spiders clambered up the bedposts, prickly arms marching toward me. All around me the blanket was a sea of twitching legs and glittering eyes.

But they weren't here for me. As the light went on, they began to pour across the floor and drop down from the ceiling. They converged on the door in a skittering swarm.

I had killed their mother . . . and they were here for mine.

ABI SLONE

Stuck in the Middle

On the basement stairs, halfway between the darkness below and the light of the first floor, Erin heard the footsteps behind her. As she took another step forward, the footsteps got louder. Like they were closer. Like they were running. Like they were on her.

On her next step she turned around and looked back into the dark. Erin could hear nothing but her own heart pounding. Turning back toward the light, she felt a chill run through her as her body was pushed ever so slightly forward. And looking up one last time, she saw the door at the top of the stairs close and heard the lock click.

JOSEPH DELANEY

All Fingers and Thumbs!

The bone witch chained my legs to a stake very close to the pit and left me there. When I tried to pick the lock, I was all fingers and thumbs.

The sun was setting behind Crow Wood, the shadows lengthening. Down in the darkness of the pit I could hear something moving. Something big and scary grunting and snuffling. Suddenly it sniffed loudly three times and growled.

"My son's hungry," said the witch. She was back and was standing behind me. "So I'll give you a chance. Feed him a morsel, one each day for ten days, and I'll let you go. Something tasty so that he won't bother to climb out. You could walk free then."

"I've nothing to feed it with!" I complained, starting to tremble.

"Oh, yes you have!" said the witch, placing a sharp knife at my side. She laughed wickedly, and the crows took flight.

"Start with your left thumb. . . ."

Then the footsteps came toward me.

ALAN GRATZ

Don't Wet the Bed

Russell's parents told him there was nothing under his bed, but he didn't believe them.

Yes, his father had turned on the lights and lifted the bedsheets off the floor to show him nothing was there, but the thing that lived under his bed came back when the lights were off. He could feel it, sense it, as surely as if it were a part of him, and he knew that no matter where he tried to climb out of bed, it could reach out and get him.

It had tentacles.

As long as Russell stayed perfectly still under his covers, as long as a foot or a hand didn't stray off the edge during the night, he was safe until morning.

The problem was, Russell had to go to the bathroom. Bad.

Last time he had wet the bed rather than put his foot

down in the dark, but tonight he was ready. The fishing rod with the straightened coat hanger on the end wobbled as he aimed for the light switch at the far end of the room, but it reached. The hook caught the switch, it started to lift—

—and the coat hanger broke through its tape and fell too far away to reach.

The light was still off, and Russell had to pee so badly now, it burned. The bathroom was just a few steps away. Maybe if he jumped, got a running start. He couldn't sleep in a wet bed again. Couldn't face the shame of telling his mother.

He stood, shivering, and backed up on his bed. Beneath him, the thing stirred.

Run as fast as you can, then jump, grab for the light switch—

Russell ran. He jumped. His foot hit the ground—

—and he was gone.

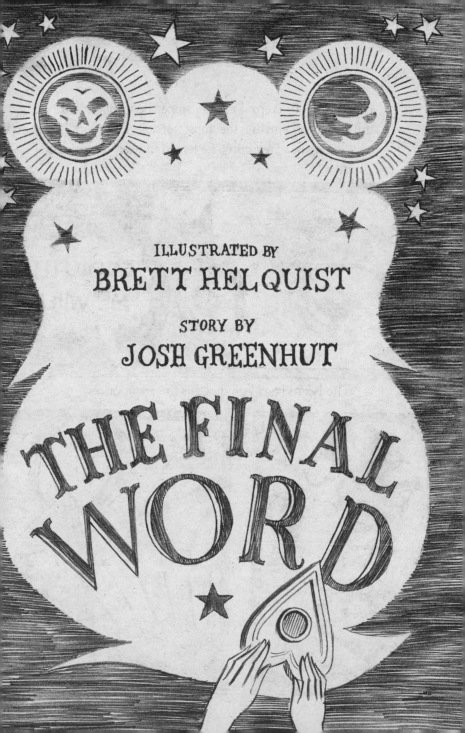

ILLUSTRATED BY

BRETT HELQUIST

STORY BY

JOSH GREENHUT

THE FINAL
WORD

It had been an eternal minute since the Ouija board had finished pronouncing the most terrible fate that Elijah could imagine. Trembling, he forced himself to ask a final question.

The board began guiding his fingers at once.

With a roar, Elijah hoisted the board over his head and brought it down against the wall with a crack. On his fourth try, it splintered. He held an edge against the floor and stamped down with his foot, hard, breaking it in half. He kept at it until the floor was littered with fragments.

Spent at last, Elijah climbed the stairs and crawled into bed. There seemed to be something hard beneath the pillow. Lifting it, he found the Ouija board—cracked and scarred, but somehow whole—staring up at him. It jerked his finger as if with a string. All the way to . . .

the third and final letter:

NEIL GAIMAN

The Shadow

It's lonely where I live, an old house a long way from anywhere. That's why I got a dog. He keeps me company.

Last night the moon was full, and it cast shadows. We took a shortcut through the woods, into the meadow beyond. I let him off leash to run. He came back holding something.

"Drop it," I ordered, and he did. I felt sick.

Somebody behind me said, "That's mine. Don't turn around."

Then the shadow beside mine was gone, and my dog whimpered in the moonlight.

LESLEY LIVINGSTON

A Day at the Lake

"It's not haunted," I had scoffed at Bradley on the way up in the car.

"Cursed, then." He'd grinned.

"You're an idiot."

Hidden Lake was cold, still, dark as a pool of spilled ink under the summer sun.

My hands, already slippery with wake spray, began to sweat on the handle grips of the towrope stretched taut between me and the ski boat. I glanced down again and felt my stomach lurch. It wasn't my imagination. Beneath me, flashes of corpse-pale bodies knifed through the murky water.

Frantically, I signaled Bradley to turn the boat back toward the shore. We were so far out. Brad—why did you take me so far out?

Sightless eyes glared up at me. Patient. Waiting.

Bradley turned the boat in a slow, lazy circle and headed in, unaware. The shore beckoned. Only a hundred yards more to the beach. The towline jerked in my hands and went slack as the ski boat's motor sputtered, spat blue smoke, and died. And I began to sink.

JON SCIESZKA

Whispered

Oh man, we never should have listened to them.
"There's nothing under the bed," they said.
"Those noises are just the wind," they said.
"It's just your imagination," they said.
We never should have listened to them.
Now *shhhhhhh* . . .

FOUND & ENVISIONED BY
VLADIMIR RADUNSKY

A Disturbing Limerick

There was a young man of Bengal
Who was asked to a fancy-dress ball
He murmured: I'll risk it—
I'll go as a biscuit.

But the dog ate him up in the hall.

ALISON McGHEE

Through the Veil

I was eleven years old when I dreamed that I became my own shadow, and that I was following my body through a dark wood. The moon was our only light, and as the woods grew deeper, it became clear that I was in danger of losing my body. You are only a shadow, a voice whispered in my ear. Without your body you cannot exist. The woods grew deeper, and the fitful light of the moon flickered among the dark branches looming above my head. My body was walking ahead of me, faster and faster. Without your body you cannot exist, came the voice again. And then it came to me that I was not dreaming, and that the moon had disappeared entirely. My body was far ahead, running. Running away from me. Help me! Help me! I tried to scream, but without my body I had no voice. I tried to run, but I had no legs. I tried to fly, but I had no wings. Help me—help—but no one heard me.

It was too late. I no longer existed.

DANIEL EHRENHAFT

The Rash

Friday afternoon, during final period, his right cheek began to itch.

He scratched softly and felt two small bumps. By the time the ball rang, his cheek was on fire. He hurried to the boys' room and saw that the two bumps had turned to seven—bumps the size of beestings. The right side of his face was a splotchy red mess.

No worries, he thought. He would rub some lotion on the itch, and it would be all cleared up by Monday morning. Just in time for the college interview. He hadn't planned on going out this weekend anyway. He'd skip the dance. He'd study and take care of this. He had to look his best Monday. He had to project success.

When he got home, seven bumps had turned to eleven.

At dinner, his left cheek began to itch, too. Mom told him not to scratch it. Scratching could lead to infection. Dad blamed it on stress: the college interview, homework, sports, friends, girls. His sister snickered. He'd never get a prom date now.

That night, the itch spread across his face and down his neck. The burning was constant, excruciating. Nothing helped—no creams or pills. Saturday, Mom and Dad called the family doctor; if it hadn't cleared up by Sunday, he should go to a hospital. He hid in his room instead. He hated hospitals. His sister avoided him, frightened of catching it. The itch would clear up; it had to. He couldn't reschedule the college interview. It was too late—

But Monday morning, after a fitful sleep, the itch was gone.

He ran his fingers over his cheeks. The flesh was cool and smooth. He smiled, stumbling out of bed. Project success, he thought. He turned on the bathroom light and looked in the mirror.

His bleary eyes stared back. He blinked once, twice.

The face belonged to someone else.

MELISSA MARR

Where Nightmares Walk

The green glow of eyes and sulfurous breath shimmer in the fog as the Nightmares come into range. The horses' steel-sharp hooves rip furrows in the field, trampling everything in their path.

"Over here!" my companion dog calls out to them, exposing me.

I didn't know he could speak, but there is no mistaking the source of the sound—or the fact that I am trapped in a field with Nightmares bearing down upon me.

The dog shakes, and his glamour falls away like water flung from his fur. Under his disguise, my helpmate is a skeletal beast with holes where its eyes should be.

"*Run*," it growls, "so we can chase."

I want to, but much like the rest of the things I want my legs to do, running is no longer an option. If I could still run, I wouldn't be alone on the night when Nightmares walk free. If I could still run, I'd be out in costume trick-or-treating with my friends.

"I can't run."

I hobble toward an oak that stands like a shadow in the fog.

The monstrous dog doesn't stop me as I drop my crutches and pull myself onto the lowest branch. It doesn't stop me as I try to heave myself higher.

"Faster!" it calls out to the Nightmares, which are almost upon me.

The only question left to answer is whether their running or my climbing is quicker.

CHRIS RASCHKA

On a Tuesday During
That Time of Year

On a Tuesday during that time of year when it is particularly unpleasant to be out in the early gray twilight of those sometimes rainy or even sleety days, a small boy, perhaps nine or ten years old, was looking in his deep sock drawer for a particular pair of warm ones that he saved for just this sort of morning. He dug past his long basketball socks, pushed aside his black dress socks, and held for a minute a pair of red-and-blue-striped socks that he had once worn to a party. Plunging his hand back into the spaghetti bowl of stockings, he felt and pinched everything, with his eyes closed, to test if it was that wonderful soft and homey wool of the pair he was looking for.

Figuring that they were perhaps in the laundry, he was about to give up when he touched something hard, lumpy, and, he thought, a little bit hairy. Curious, he curled his fingers around whatever it was and slowly pulled it up, the layers of socks tumbling this way and that, until when he opened his hand he found something gray-green, longish—about five inches—and thin, scabby with little hillocks crowned by short black hairs, very wrinkled, and with what looked like withered corn husk protruding from its end.

It was a finger.

STACEY GODENIR

Death Rides a Pink Bicycle

Calvin walked home from school thinking about how much he hated his kid sister, Annie. She was skipping beside him, humming some ridiculous kindergarten song and embarrassing him as usual. He was about to tell her to shut up when a little blond girl, riding a bright pink bicycle, raced by, knocking him off the sidewalk.

"Watch it!" he hollered after the girl as she stopped at the street corner ahead.

Slowly, the girl craned her neck toward Calvin until he could see her face. Or rather, what should have been her face.

Instead, bits of pink, doughy flesh hung from a bleached skull. Black eye sockets, empty as a bottomless pit, stared back at Calvin.

The skeleton pointed a bony finger at the terrified boy,

then turned and pedaled the pink bicycle into the street.

Bam!

The garbage truck that smashed into her didn't even hit the brakes.

Calvin ran to the corner, dragging Annie behind him, but there was nothing there. No girl, no bicycle—nothing.

By the time they got home, Calvin had just about convinced himself that he had imagined the whole thing. That is, until he saw his dad unloading a bright pink bicycle from the car. It was the one little blond-haired Annie had been asking for.

Suddenly, Calvin knew what he had seen. It was death riding the pink bicycle. His sister's death.

He realized that he didn't hate Annie after all—just the opposite. So Calvin jumped on the bicycle and bolted into the street. Desperate to save his sister, he didn't even look where he was going. Which is why he didn't see the garbage truck heading his way.

DAN GUTMAN

I'm Not Afraid

I'm not afraid of the dark.

So when I climbed the rotting steps of the old Granger Mansion on Halloween night and peeked through the broken window, it didn't bother me that there were no lights on.

When the squeaky wooden door opened by itself, it didn't scare me.

When the echoing voice invited me inside to take some Halloween candy, it didn't scare me.

When I stepped across the threshold and the door closed behind me, it didn't scare me.

When I heard the lock click shut, it didn't scare me.

The creaking floorboards didn't scare me.

The cobwebs brushing my face didn't scare me.

The portraits of old people hanging on the walls didn't scare me.

The knife that was sitting on the player piano didn't scare me.

The strange chemical smell didn't scare me.

The otherworldly sounds coming from an unseen violin didn't scare me.

The acrid taste in my mouth didn't scare me.

The tortured screaming coming from a distant room didn't scare me.

The footsteps that kept getting closer . . . and closer . . . didn't scare me.

The insect crawling up the back of my leg didn't scare me.

The blood that was dripping down the walls didn't scare me.

No, none of that stuff scared me.

I'll tell you what scared me.

It was the clown.

ALICE KUIPERS

The Doll

When my stepmum, Angela, gave me a doll, my dad told me I had to say thank you. I said thank you, sweet as a sour apple. The glint in Angela's eyes was wicked. But Dad didn't see it.

I found the doll on my pillow with a pin in its tummy. My stomachache was so bad, I didn't have the strength to throw the doll off the bed. By morning I managed to pull out the pin. I carried the doll to breakfast. My stepmum said, "How did you sleep?"

"Like a baby," I said. Anyone with half a brain could have seen her surprise. But not Dad.

He cut in. "What are you going to call it?"

I had to think for only a second. I twiddled the pin in my fingers.

"Angela," I said. I smiled at the horror in her eyes.

Dad thought that was sweet.

As a sour apple.

FRANK VIVA

Easy Over

He was trapped in this hot, dark place. No mother. Every day was the same. He was very sad. Little by little, the scorching heat worked its way into his skin. He hated the stinging smoke. He hated the greasy fingers. No amount of scrubbing could wash away the bad smell. This was his life. Soon it would be over.

DEADPAN

LIBBA BRAY

Them

Amir had run far and fast, and his breath burned in his lungs. His shirt was spattered with blood from where one of them had gotten close and Mr. Johnson had killed it. Poor Mr. Johnson.

On the radio, they'd said it would take days before they reached Parkersville. But the next afternoon, the radio had gone to static, and when his mother didn't return from her job, Amir went to look for her.

He saw shattered windows, burning buildings, bloody handprints on a car's hood. At the corner of Main and Oak, Leo Black's bike lay on its side, the wheels still spinning. The radio reports said they could hide anywhere, and some had already adapted, learned to track and hunt rather than just attack. You never saw those coming. You'd only hear a low, syrupy sound, and then it was too late.

As Amir crossed the park, his luck ran out. Hordes of them lurched from their hiding places and came after him. Oh, the sunken, lifeless eyes! Sharp teeth. Rotting flesh. Mouths moving hungrily. One grabbed his arm. Then came Mr. Johnson with his baseball bat, poor Mr. Johnson screaming as Amir ran for home.

It was dusk now. He opened the door. The kitchen light shone. His mother's coat hung on the back of her chair.

"Mom!" he called, running.

He slipped and fell. The floor was slick with blood. And the shadows reverberated with a deep gurgle.

JOYCE CAROL OATES

Tiger Kitty

Tiger Kitty was my favorite! Tiger Kitty came into our family when I was four years old.

Tiger Kitty slept with me, cuddled and purred in the crook of my arm. Tiger Kitty had the prettiest soft orange-stripe fur, a tail with a white tip, and a little white nose with a single freckle.

One day when it was very windy, Tiger Kitty went away into the woods behind our house. We called and called Tiger Kitty, but he didn't come back for a day and a night and another day and a night, and then one morning there was Tiger Kitty by the back door mewing to be let inside—we were so happy, we kissed and hugged him.

Tiger Kitty was very happy to be home! Tiger Kitty gobbled up all the food in his dish and mewed for more.

Some change had taken place in Tiger Kitty in the

woods. He was longer than he'd been but skinnier, and his eyes were a strange tawny yellow. His tail had a funny bump in it, as if it had been broken, and the white tip seemed to have faded. The freckle seemed to have faded from his nose also.

Sometimes when I pet Tiger Kitty, he doesn't seem to know who I am and hisses and claws at me—if I'm not quick, Tiger Kitty will scratch my hand. But a few seconds later Tiger Kitty recognizes me, and purrs and rubs hard against my ankles.

Especially when he's hungry, Tiger Kitty purrs and rubs against my ankles.

Tiger Kitty sleeps with me like always. Though in his sleep Tiger Kitty sometimes growls and twitches, and at such times I am afraid he might scratch me if I woke him.

I love Tiger Kitty!—but there is a secret between us no one else knows.

If you guess our secret, don't say it out loud. Tiger Kitty can *scratch*.

JONATHAN LETHEM

Inventory

11 upper arms (one with annoying "MOM" tattoo,
one with chafed elbow)

7 lower arms, 3 complete with wrist and hand (one
with only three fingers)

5 various torso components (some potential here,
I think)

8 thighs (two atrociously hairy)

9 calves with knees

5 heads (one bald and quite ugly, sorry)

1 foot (??? someone stealing feet?)

also various rejected noses and ears, lost count

jar of eyeballs

Note to secretary of acquisitions:
MUST REFRESH INVENTORY!!!!

MICHAEL CONNELLY

Shortcut

The shortcut took me down into the wooded valley on the other side of the railroad tracks. It was dark down here, because the tall trees created a canopy the sun could not penetrate. It had not been raining, but now water dripped down on me from above. The air was damp, and the plants at ground level seemed huge, some of them with leaves as big as elephant ears.

No one ever cut through here. It was off-limits. But I was late. Very late. The rumor was that there was a tunnel that went directly under the railroad embankment and that it would knock fifteen minutes off my time getting home.

The path grew narrow as it led me farther down. Soon the leaves and branches of the bushes scraped at my arms. And then I finally saw the tunnel. Its opening was dark and lined with whitewashed bricks. As I got closer, I saw tangles of roots hanging down from inside.

I saw no light and thought the rumor couldn't be true. The tunnel didn't go through. But then I felt warm air come out of the darkness and wash over me. If there was air coming through, then there had to be an opening on the other side.

I checked my watch. I was out of time. I stepped into the tunnel and ducked under the hanging roots. My second step landed on something soft. It moved and jerked my foot out from under me. I fell, and my hands felt the slime. That was when I realized that the tunnel entrance wasn't lined with white bricks.

They were teeth.

LAUREN MYRACLE

Strawberry Bubbles

Earlier, before we heard the window shatter, I sat on the closed toilet seat and kept Amy company while she took her bath. I poured in her strawberry bubble bath, and I moved the razor from the edge of the tub. I thought, How stupid to keep a razor in a child's bathroom.

It wasn't a safety razor like my mom's; it was an old-fashioned razor with an exposed blade that gleamed. I touched it ever so lightly—just to see—and a bead of shiny red bubbled up on the pad of my finger.

Now I fight to keep Amy from running downstairs.

"Scribbles!" she whispers, struggling against me. "We have to get Scribbles!"

"Amy, no." I can hardly breathe, and my thrumming pulse is making me dizzy. Th-*thump*, th-*thump*. So loud in my head I can barely hear . . . what? Or rather, who?

Who is downstairs, prowling the rooms of this cold, dark house?

Not Amy's parents, who aren't due for hours. And not Scribbles, Amy's poor dumb bunny who comes out of his hutch only when Amy unlatches the top and scoops him up, holding him like a baby in her pudgy four-year-old arms.

Only, if you squeezed a baby that hard, the baby would cry. Scribbles never makes a sound.

"He's my bunny!" Amy wails. "He needs me!"

She twists free and darts out of the bathroom—the smallest, most tucked-away room on the second floor, and so the best place to hide. But to hide, you have to stay put. To stay safe, you cannot go seeking.

But I am the babysitter. I have no choice.

This time, when I pick up the razor, I hold the blade away from me. At the last minute, I also grab the plastic princess container of bubble bath. I don't know why. Yet the heft of it gives me courage.

"Amy?" I call hoarsely.

God, it's dark. I don't want to go down this dark hall . . . these dark stairs. . . .

But I am the babysitter.

I reach the kitchen. Someone breathes by the rabbit hutch.

"Amy?"

Then the screaming begins, high-pitched and piercing.

"Amy? *Amy!*"

I slap the wall to find the light switch. I flip it on, and a stranger has Amy. Dangling from his other hand, hind legs thrashing wildly, is Scribbles—and it's Scribbles, not Amy, whose animal fear makes this horrible shriek.

"Rabbits scream when they're in mortal terror," the stranger says in a velvety, dreadful voice. "Did you know that?"

I stare into his soulless eyes.

He chuckles. "Little girls scream, too. When I make them." He digs his bony fingers into Amy's chubby arm, and she whimpers.

But I am the babysitter.

I feint as if to slash him. When he dodges, I'm ready with the plastic princess. I aim. I squeeze. *And now who's screaming, you soulless monster?*

His hands fly to his burning eyes and Amy flees, pausing only long enough to scoop up her stupid, precious bunny.

"Run!" I cry.

As soon as they're out the back door and running for

the neighbors, I squirt the remaining bubble bath on the tiled kitchen floor. When this monster comes after us, half blind, he will fall. And he won't smell blood, as he had hoped, but strawberry bubbles.

BARRY YOURGRAU

We Think You Do

On a dare two boys sneak into a spooky house. They gulp at the vast cobwebs, the shadows.

There's a moan from upstairs.

"*Help.* . . ."

The boys gasp. They rush back to the window they snuck through. But then one of them decides to investigate. Cursing, his buddy flees.

Heart pounding, the lone boy edges up the main stairs. He reaches a dark doorway. Trembling, he peers in. He gasps in shock.

A life-size replica of himself stands tied up in the bare room, a rope around its neck.

"*Help* . . . ," it moans mechanically.

The stairs creak below. "Ah," chuckles a sinister voice. "Here to exchange places? Your buddy is my new assistant.

He's very talented, don't you think?"

That's how the town starts to fill with replicas. You know some of them, too.

No?

Well, here in the spooky house, we think you do.

AARON RENIER

The Prisoner of Eternia

SOMETHING was ALIVE and IMPRISONED in my wall.

HISSSSSSSSSS

The ring... its LIGHT, must've woke it.

FWAAA

Who trapped it in there? Was it... DANGEROUS?

Did my mom know about it? Was she hiding it from me?

HIIISSSSS

My mom says the growl is just the furnace.

But I know better.

renier

GREGORY MAGUIRE

In Conclusion

You turn the page in the anthology of nightmares. Your head throbs. At least this is the last story.

But you begin to anticipate—the way one does—the infamous two words centered in boldface type. Farther on.

Don't look. Don't dare glance ahead. You will come to them in time. We all do.

They wait for us.

That omega prophecy curses the turn of the page. Inevitable. Final. What if—when you get there—you find out the truth of this bedeviled book—that those words mean what they say. They really are . . .

THE END.

Index

SUSAN RICH

art by Lisa Brown

has edited a frightening number of books, including those in Lemony Snicket's A Series of Unfortunate Events, Gloria Whelan's National Book Award–winning *Homeless Bird*, and the series Flat Stanley's Worldwide Adventures. Born in Winnipeg, she attended McGill University in Montreal and received her master's degree in children's literature from Simmons College in Boston. She has haunted old publishing houses in New York and then Toronto, where she now lives with her devilish husband and ghastly children.

Half-Minute Horrors
is published in partnership
with First Book.

First Book provides new books to children in need, addressing one of the most important factors affecting literacy: access to books. The nonprofit First Book has distributed more than 65 million free and low-cost books to children in need and the programs that serve them in thousands of communities. First Book envisions a world where all children have an enriched learning environment with new books and educational resources of their own. Find out more at www.firstbook.org.